Emily Martin

ILLUSTRATED BY Mara Shaughnessy

downpour

SKY PONY PRESS
NEW YORK

It rained for days
until poppies ran.

Their red first
ran down stem
and leaves.

Then, red, the roots,
Red, the ground,
Red, the stones sitting around.
Red, the grass underfoot.

Red, the beaks of curious birds.

Red, the field where sit the poppies.

Red, the fence around the field.

Red, the road beyond the fence.

Red, the gravel hiding the road.

Red, on the corner, a puddle, and toad.

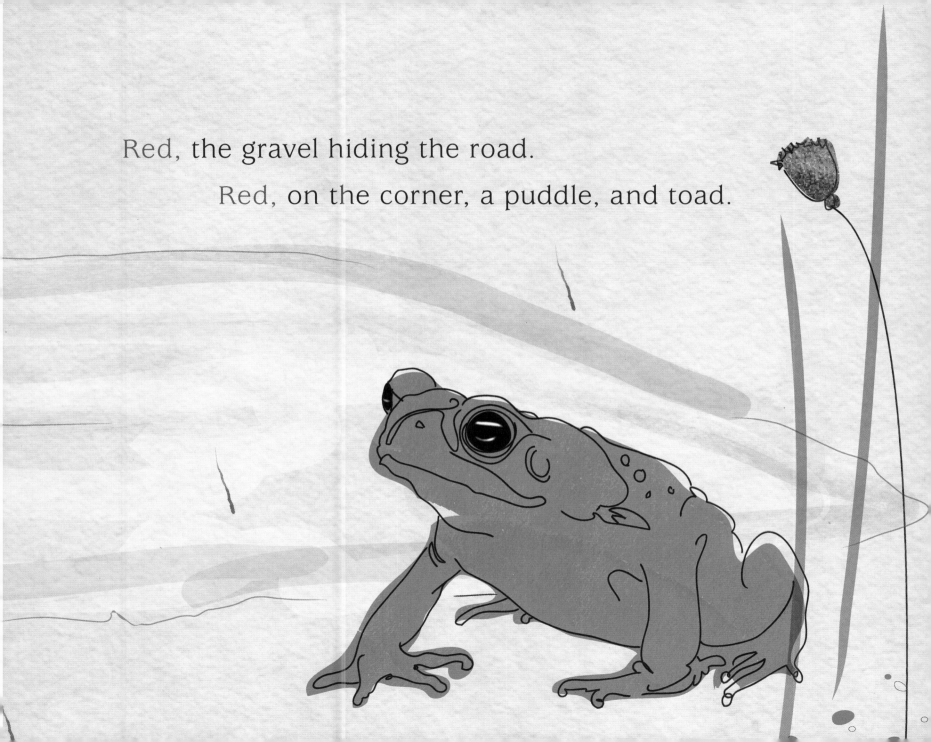

Red, out of its bed, the river.
Red, the toes of hurried foxes.

Red, the little bush's thorns.

Red, the beating hearts of bees.

Red, the sleepy black ram's horns.

Red, the happy old man's beard.

Red,

the

hedgehog's

prickly

hair.

Red, the mosses, lichen, and fern.

Red, the big wheel
at the faraway fair.

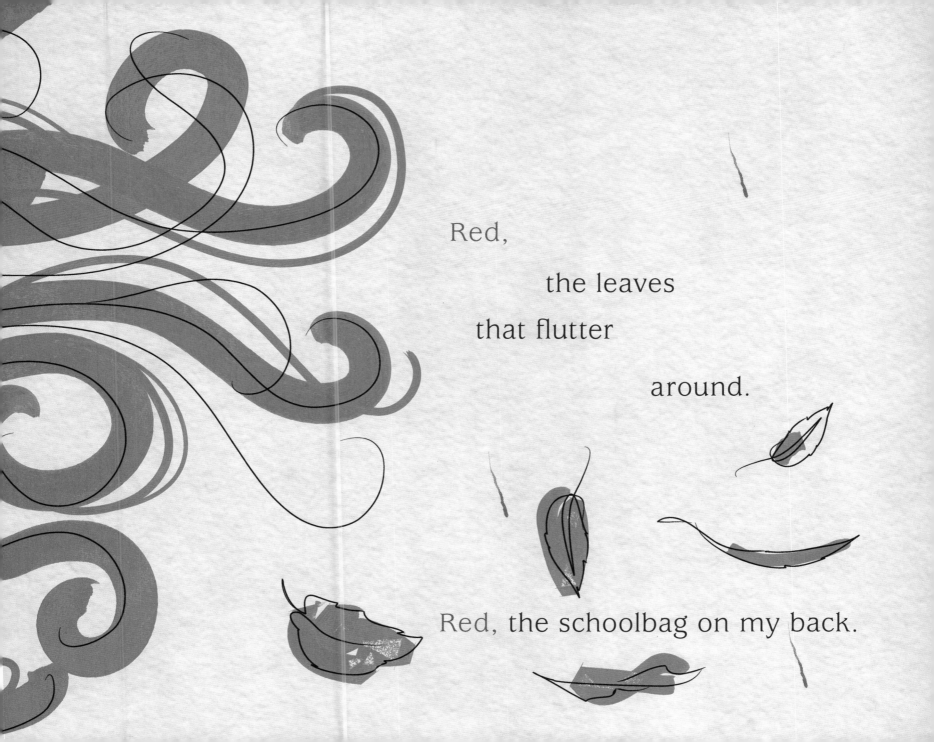

Red,

the leaves

that flutter

around.

Red, the schoolbag on my back.

Red, the big bus turning the corner.

Red, the school children waving goodbye.

Red,

the hedgehog's

noisy snores.

Red, the fish, their shiny scales.

Red, the foam on the sandy shore.

Red, the little river's light.

Red, everything in the eyes of butterflies,

But poor poppies now turned white.

To Claire Juliette, my daughter, who
learned how to laugh yesterday.

\* \* \*

Poetry lurks, especially in the rain.

Red used to be my least favorite color.
Only fools don't change their minds.

Disaster is inevitable. Watch it unfold,
find beauty.

## Acknowledgments:

To Mara Shaughnessy whose boundless
imagination and able hand brought
this small monsoon to life, I am much
indebted. To my outstanding editor,
Jennifer McCartney, who gave this
tale a home, my deepest gratitude.
To my parents and sister, who are still
puzzled — but forgiving — over my
creative endeavors, thank you for your
patience. To Clara, whose unparalleled
generosity and kind heart have often
kept me afloat, thank you. And most
importantly, to my husband Scott, whose
unfailing love and support have allowed
me the luxury of creating this moment
and many others, I am forever beholden.

Text © 2013 Emily Martin
Illustrations © 2013 Mara Shaughnessy
Book design by Natalie Olsen, Kisscut Design

Sky Pony Press books may be purchased in bulk
at special discounts for sales promotion, corporate
gifts, fund-raising, or educational purposes.
Special editions can also be created to specifications.
For details, contact the Special Sales Department,
Sky Pony Press, 307 West 36th Street, 11th Floor,
New York, NY 10018 or info@skyhorsepublishing.com.

Sky Pony® is a registered trademark of Skyhorse
Publishing, Inc.®, a Delaware corporation.

Visit our website at **www.skyponypress.com**.

10 9 8 7 6 5 4 3 2 1

*Library of Congress Cataloging-in-Publication Data available on file*

Manufactured in China, January 2013

This product conforms to CPSIA 2008